The Secret of the CIRCLE-K CAVE

by Anna Jane Hays

illustrated by Jerry Smath

Kane Press, I
New York

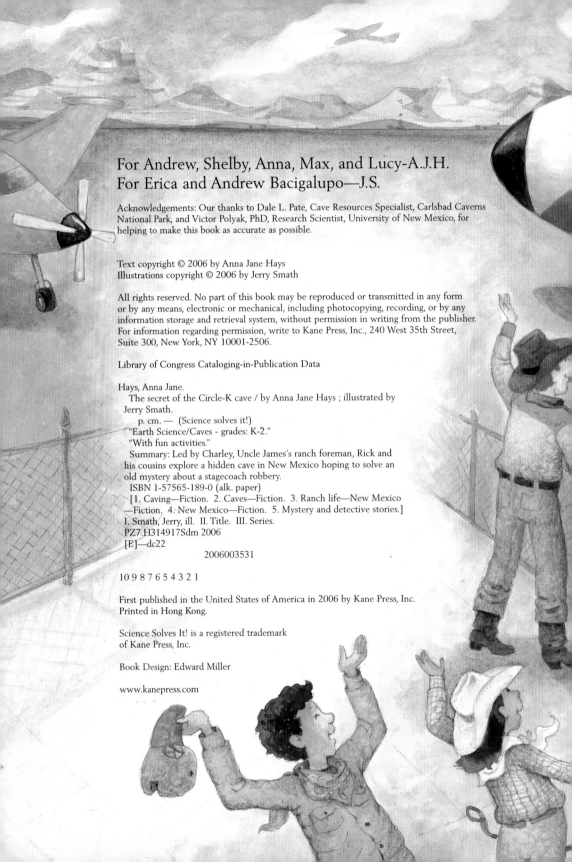

For Andrew, Shelby, Anna, Max, and Lucy-A.J.H.
For Erica and Andrew Bacigalupo—J.S.

Acknowledgements: Our thanks to Dale L. Pate, Cave Resources Specialist, Carlsbad Caverns
National Park, and Victor Polyak, PhD, Research Scientist, University of New Mexico, for
helping to make this book as accurate as possible.

Text copyright © 2006 by Anna Jane Hays
Illustrations copyright © 2006 by Jerry Smath

Library of Congress Cataloging-in-Publication Data

Hays, Anna Jane.
   The secret of the Circle-K cave / by Anna Jane Hays ; illustrated by
Jerry Smath.
     p. cm. — (Science solves it!)
   "Earth Science/Caves - grades: K-2."
   "With fun activities."
   Summary: Led by Charley, Uncle James's ranch foreman, Rick and
his cousins explore a hidden cave in New Mexico hoping to solve an
old mystery about a stagecoach robbery.
   ISBN 1-57565-189-0 (alk. paper)
   [1. Caving—Fiction. 2. Caves—Fiction. 3. Ranch life—New Mexico
—Fiction. 4. New Mexico—Fiction. 5. Mystery and detective stories.]
I. Smath, Jerry, ill. II. Title. III. Series.
PZ7.H314917Sdm 2006
[E]—dc22
                    2006003531

10 9 8 7 6 5 4 3 2 1

First published in the United States of America in 2006 by Kane Press, Inc.
Printed in Hong Kong.

Science Solves It! is a registered trademark
of Kane Press, Inc.

Book Design: Edward Miller

www.kanepress.com

"Hey, RICK! Over here!"

Aunt Ida and Uncle James were calling to him. Joe Bob and Betsy were waving wildly.

Rick took a deep breath of desert air. This was his first trip out West, and he was ready for adventure!

3

The minute they reached the Circle-K
Ranch, Betsy pulled Rick toward the corral.
   "We'll show you around!" said Joe Bob.
   Charley, the ranch foreman, helped Rick
saddle up—and they were off!
   Rick smiled. It was good to see his cousins
again.

As they rode out toward the mesa, Rick stared at the mountains. They glowed like gold in the late afternoon light.

"This way, Rick," Betsy called. "I want to show you something."

A **mesa** is a steep hill with a flat top like a table.

"Here's our magic stream," said Betsy. She dropped a twig boat into the water.

"It *vanished!*" Rick said. "Where did it go?"

Just then Joe Bob shouted, "Hound Dog! Where are you, boy?"

"There he goes." Rick pointed toward some bushes. "He's chasing a bunny."

Betsy laughed. "That was a jackrabbit, silly!"

With a yelp, Hound Dog jumped out of a hole in the cliff wall. *WHISH!* A flock of fuzzy, brown creatures flew out after him and zoomed off overhead.

"BATS!" Rick yelled. "Do they bite? Do they *suck blood?*"

Betsy giggled. "Bats eat insects, not people."

The kids peeked into the dark opening and felt cool air brush against their faces.

"It's a *cave*," said Rick.

Betsy looked excited. "Can we go in?"

"Sorry, but it's almost sunset," said Joe Bob. "We'd better ride back."

Limestone caves are formed when water seeps underground and eats away at rock. When the water drains out, it leaves behind a hollow—a cave. This takes thousands of years!

"We found a CAVE!" Rick hollered.

"This *is* cave country," said Uncle James. "The famous Carlsbad Caverns aren't far from here."

"I've stumbled onto a few caves myself," said Charley. "Explored them, too."

"Will you help us explore ours?" asked Betsy.

"Sure," Charley said. "We'll go into town tomorrow for supplies."

Rick couldn't wait.

The next morning, Charley took the kids to the old Thunderbird Trading Post.

"This is right out of a movie!" said Rick.

Charley gathered up hardhats and ropes and flashlights.

Joe Bob tossed candy bars into a basket. "For energy," he explained.

What Cavers Wear
• protective pants and shirt • sturdy boots • gloves • hardhat with light and chinstrap • backpack for supplies

"Check this out, Rick." Betsy pointed to an old poster. "There were real stagecoach robbers around here."

"Wonder if they ever got caught," said Rick.

"Nope," replied Charley. "And nobody even knows for sure if they really did it."

WANTED!
THADDEUS AND THOMAS BARTON
THE BARTON BOYS
STAGECOACH ROBBERY
GUADALUPE PASS, JUNE 15, 1860
REWARD!

What Cavers Carry
• flashlights and extra batteries
• food and water • first-aid kit • map
of cave • compass • rope and climbing
gear for experienced cavers

11

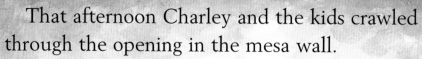

That afternoon Charley and the kids crawled
through the opening in the mesa wall.

Rick was the last to stand up in a small, dark
room. "Any b-b-bats hanging out in here?"

"Don't go batty on us," Joe Bob teased him.

"No problem," said Rick. "I'm good to go."

Cave Rules
Always go with at least two other
cavers—never alone. Do not touch or
step on any rock formations. Take
out everything you brought in.

Betsy shined her flashlight on the wall.
"T. & T. B. What does that mean?"

"Thaddeus and Thomas Barton?" said Joe Bob.

"The Barton Boys!" said Rick. "Maybe they stashed the stagecoach loot in here!"

"Maybe," said Charley. "Look at this message."

"Smart and brave. That's us!" yelled Rick.

T. & T. B.

TO FIND
THE SECRET OF THE CAVE
YOU MUST BE STRONG
& SMART & BRAVE!

"Stick together, spelunkers!" Charley called as they crawled deeper into the cave.

"I hope there aren't any creepy-crawlies down here," thought Rick.

"I hope this leads to the gold," thought Betsy.

"I hope Charley didn't forget the candy bars," thought Joe Bob.

Spelunka is the Latin word for *cave*. Cave explorers are called *spelunkers* (spih•LUNG•kerz). But most like to be called *cavers*.

Hound Dog pawed at Joe Bob. "What's that, boy?" Joe Bob pulled a pouch from the dog's mouth. Out fell a brass key and a gold coin! "The treasure *must* be here!"

The cavers walked faster now. When they came to a fork, they chose a path quickly and pushed on—until a huge boulder blocked the way.

Joe Bob groaned. "Dead end."

"That's it for today, kids," said Charley.

Back above ground, the kids sat around a campfire and rested from their long day. The sun slipped behind the mesa as they toasted marshmallows and drank hot chocolate.

"Will you tell us the story of the robbery?" Rick asked Charley.

"Well," said Charley, "the legend goes that the Barton Boys were seen riding this way the day the stagecoach was robbed. Then they just disappeared—as if swallowed up by a hole in the ground."

"The Circle-K cave!" the kids yelled.

Early the next day the spelunkers crawled back into the cave. They headed straight to the fork.

"Hey!" called Betsy. "Doesn't this rock look like it's pointing to the path on the left?"

"Yes!" said Joe Bob excitedly. "Let's go!"

They crept into the tunnel.

Caves stay at around the same temperature all year. That means they usually feel cool in the summer and warm in the winter!

"*Shhhh!*" Charley whispered. He pointed to a family of bats hanging above them.

Rick stayed close to Hound Dog. "I just won't look up," he told himself.

The cavers silently tiptoed on until the path opened up into a large chamber.

Bats like the "twilight zone" of caves—where it's not totally dark. Unless they're bothered, bats sleep in caves all day and fly out to eat insects at night.

Charley flicked on his big lantern.
"Wow!" said Betsy. "This is amazing."
Stone curtains draped the walls. A rock
chandelier hung from the ceiling. A high
waterfall splashed into a pool.

Water dripping into a cave
leaves a trail of minerals. Over
thousands of years, the drops
form rock "icicles" that hang
from the cave ceiling. These
are called **stalactites**. Minerals
that drip down from stalactites
form towers on the cave floor.
These are called **stalagmites**.

Rick forgot all about bats and creepy-crawlies. "Betsy!" he called. He had spotted something floating in the clear water. "It's your twig boat!"

"So we've found where the magic stream goes!" she said. "But no stagecoach loot."

"Over here," said Joe Bob. "Another room."

A stream aboveground may disappear suddenly when a cave "steals" its water! The water vanishes down a hole leading underground.

They entered the chamber and gasped.

There, on a stone pedestal, sat a dusty old chest. Printed on its side was BANK OF NEW MEXICO.

"The loot from the stagecoach!" Rick shouted.

"Well, whaddaya know!" said Charley.

Betsy pushed the brass key into the lock.
It squeaked and slowly turned.

Joe Bob lifted the lid.

Rick shined his flashlight inside.

"What—?"

"It's another coin!" said Betsy. "And a note!"

Dear T & T,
Who is strong
and brave
and smart?
Little brother,
Bart

"Looks like there was a third Barton Boy," said Charley.

"And he stole the treasure from his big brothers!" added Joe Bob.

"But *we* solved the mystery!" said Rick.

The next morning, the cavers plunked the dusty chest down on Sheriff Bill High's desk.

His mouth dropped open. "The strongbox from the stagecoach robbery!"

The spelunkers told him how they had found the chest deep in the Circle-K cave.

"So, the Barton Boys really did it," said Sheriff High. "And their weasely little brother Bart grabbed the loot!"

BANK
OF
NEW MEXICO

The very same day, Sheriff High called a press conference on the courthouse steps. "I'd like to thank these brave cave explorers," he told the crowd. "They solved a famous old mystery."

He turned to Joe Bob, Betsy, and Rick and pinned a star badge on each one's shirt. "I appoint you Deputy Sheriffs of Eddy County!"

Rick and his cousins beamed.

That evening, Rick started packing.

"Is it okay if I leave my caving gear for the next time I visit?" he asked Aunt Ida.

"Of course, Deputy Rick," she said. "And take this newspaper with you to show everybody back East."

"But don't pack the candy bar," said Joe Bob. "You'll need it tomorrow for our *big* cave adventure!"

CARLSBAD CURRENT ARGUS

STAGE ROBBERY SOLVED! YOUNG EXPLORERS FIND CLUES IN SECRET CAVE

EVIDENCE GOES TO CARLSBAD MUSEUM

On Rick's last day in New Mexico, his family took him to the Carlsbad Caverns.

"Awesome!" Rick pointed to the towering rock formations.

In 1901, a cowboy named Jim White became the first person known to explore the Carlsbad Caverns. But rock paintings at the entrance prove that people had been there thousands of years ago.

"Just like in the Circle-K cave, only bigger!" said Betsy.

"*Way* bigger!" said Joe Bob.

Carlsbad Caverns became a U.S. National Park in 1930. They are famous for their large size and spectacular rock formations. The caverns are now visited by thousands of people every year.

It was time for Rick to say goodbye.

Betsy gave him a big hug. "There are more mysteries to solve around here," she said.

"Right," said Joe Bob. "It's your duty as Deputy Sheriff to come back."

Rick smiled. He was already planning his next visit.

THINK LIKE A SCIENTIST

Rick and his cousins think like scientists—and so can you!
Scientists are like detectives. They hunt for clues, study the information, and *draw conclusions* about the world around them.

Look Back

- On pages 7 and 8, what conclusion do the kids draw from the bats and the cool air coming from the opening in the cliff wall?
- When Rick spots the twig boat on page 21, what conclusion does Betsy draw about the magic stream?

Try This!

Draw a cave conclusion!
Look at the pictures below. How are stalactites and stalagmites formed? (Hint: Read the sidebar on page 20.) Now study the last picture. What conclusion can you draw about how columns are formed?

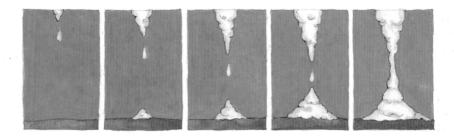

Spelunkers on the Move! Did you know that caves have been discovered in 48 of the 50 states? The nearest cave might be closer than you think. Check it out!